pocket.watch™

Love Diana

The Princess Handbook

This book belongs to:

_____

Library of Congress Control Number: 2021948097
ISBN 978-0-06-320440-9

22 23 24 25 26   TC   10 9 8 7 6 5 4 3 2 1

First Edition

When cooking, it is important to keep safety in mind. Children should always ask permission from an
adult before cooking and should be supervised by an adult in the kitchen at all times. The publisher and
authors disclaim any liability from an injury that might result from the use, proper or improper, of the
recipes and activities contained in this book.

pocket.watch

Love, Diana™

the Princess Handbook

HARPER

An Imprint of HarperCollinsPublishers

Table of Contents

With love from the Land of Play!

Hello!
Do you like to use your imagination?
Me too! When I use my imagination, I go to the Land of Play—a place where anything and everything is possible. Are you ready?
Let's go!
Love, Diana xx

Introducing ... Me!

Hey, everyone, it's me, Diana! It's great to meet you! People call me the Princess of Play because I love dressing up! I also love exploring and making new friends.

9

Let's explore together.

I love to play. **Let's pretend!**

It's great to meet you!

I live with my **mom, dad, Roma**, and my baby **brother, Oliver**.

I have a really cool **Bubble Mobile.** Check it out!

Come on, **turn the page to** meet them!

Meet my family!

ME!

13

Five things I love:

Cats

Milkshakes

Unicorns

Dancing

The Color Purple

This is my Magic Trunk. It has all sorts of costumes!

I could be a **pilot** or a **soccer star**.

I could be an **artist** or a **pop singer**.

I use my imagination to become whoever I want to be. Play it, be it! **Do you want to see inside?**

Fairy Mermaid

Princess Pop Star

Superhero Astronaut

Construction Worker

My Magic Trunk is full of amazing outfits. I love to put them on and play pretend. What do you like to dress up as?

Artist

Scientist

Scuba Diver

Even Roma joins in on the fun. Check out artist Roma!

Let's be friends!

Friendships start by getting to know each other. Here are some of my preferences—what are yours?

Would you rather . . .

1 eat ice cream or candy?

2 tell the truth or do a dare?

3 swim in a pool or in the ocean?

4 live on the moon or under the sea?

5 be able to read minds or have x-ray vision?

Now presenting . . . my royal court!

Koko, the Kittycorn— isn't she the cutest?

Winston, the Dog

Bonnie,
the Bunny

Honey,
the Horse

The Land of Play

Whoosh down the slide and join me in my land of make-believe.

Meet all of my friends in the Land of Play!

Koko

Bonnie

Down the slippy slide I go!

Roma

Winston

Let's fly away!
Honey
Poppy
Boris
Hurry up, Roma!
Mom
Blubber
My Playstone
Rob

My Playstone

The **Playstone** is a magical gem that helps my imagination come to life. It's actually inside my hairbrush. When I want to go to the Land of Play, I close my eyes, wave my wand, and watch the bubbles appear!

Power of Play, take us away!

27

Royally yours

I love playing with my friends in the Land of Play.

 Let's meet them!

Koko

Koko is the cutest Kittycorn ever. She's full of fun and kindness, even though she's a bit of a scaredy cat.

Winston

Winston might be a small pup, but he's loud, brave, and always by my side helping me solve magical mysteries.

Bonnie

You'll find Bonnie the Bunny bounding across the castle grounds. Bonnie is my goofy court jester who loves ice cream—check out her ice-cream cone baton!

My friends protect me from the bad guys of Boredom Bog. **Watch out!** They may be hiding on this page . . .

Honey

Honey is my beautiful horse. Her mane and tail can change colors and she takes me on adventures in the Land of Play.

The Bad Guys of Boredom Bog

All Boris the Bore and his Minions of the Mundane want to do is ruin our fun and make everything boring. **FOREVER!**

Blubber,
the Duke of Drudgery

Diana Says!

Sorry, bad guys, **fun wins every time!**

Poppy,
the Pesky Pigeon

Boris,
the Baron of Boredom

Rob,
the Rude Raccoon

Bags of fun

My Magic Backpack carries so many things! Open it up and what do we find?

What would you put in my backpack?

Hero bows

I take it everywhere!

Playstone

Playstone transforming into my wand!

Butterfly Garden

We've had so many adventures in the Land of Play. One time we went on a butterfly mission!

1 Diana and Roma are in the **Land of Play**. Boris has drained all the **color** from the **beautiful butterflies.**

Let's save the butterflies!

2 "**The Princess of Play** and the **Prince of Pretend** are here to save them!" says Diana.

3 Diana and Roma go into the **Royal Garden**. There are so many sad butterflies. Diana reaches for her **backpack**. She has an idea!

4 Diana pulls out her chemistry set. She mixes up lots of different colors. But there's one thing missing . . .

5 Color blasters! Now they can give the butterflies back their color.

Take that, Boris!

6 Diana and Roma **fire colors into the sky** and they stick to the butterflies. It works! The butterflies have their **color back**.

7 Just when they think their work is finished, Boris tries to stop them with his **Ho-Hum Helicopter**. Diana knows just what to do. They **supercharge** their **color blasters** and send Boris packing!

Great job, Roma!

8 "**Bye-bye, boring Boris!**" Diana chuckles. The **beautiful butterflies** are back for good, and the Princess of Play has saved the day!

Friendship is the most magical thing of all!

Here are some more of my preferences—what are yours?

Would you rather . . .

1 stay up late or get up early?

2 have a pet unicorn or kitty?

3 play with kitties or puppies?

4 choose an owl or panda bear?

Get up early

Unicorn

Kitties

owl

Wand

Fancy shoes

There are so many things to do and see in the Land of Play . . . the only limit is your imagination. **Play it, be it!**

First, let's start in the **Castle**. It has so many rooms full of magic and surprises!

My dazzling and daring adventures!

You never know when you'll open a door to a room full of toys or games, a music studio, or even a royal throne fit just for me—the Princess of Play!

And look at my **Bubble Mobile!**

The Princess of Play

Backpack

Slipper

underwater fun

Diana and Roma can become scuba divers to explore the deep blue Silly Sea.

We float underwater!

I love the Silly Sea. My scuba mask helps me breathe underwater!

Come on, Diana!

Sing along

Join in on the fun and perform
Play It, Be It with me and Roma!

1

Let's make music!

I am Diana
The Princess of Play
Yeah, yeah, yeah
I wanna take you to the
    Land of Play
Yeah, yeah, yeah

2

To a magical land
Where you'll understand
The power of play is at
Your command
It's in your hands

with me

3

Chorus 1
Play it, be it
Anything is possible
Play it, be it
Your imagination rules

4

Chorus 2
Play it, be it
In my land of make-
believe
Play it, be it
Be the one you wanna be

5

Hey, Diana, what's the plan?
Who do you wanna be today?
What do you say?

6

Meet my brother, Roma,
The Prince of Pretend
Yeah, yeah, yeah
He's always with me
And so are my friends
Yeah, yeah, yeah

7

Play is the way to fight
    boredom today
Power of play, take us away
Take us away

[Repeat chorus 1]

8

Come and spend the day with me
Be the one you wanna be
Come and spend the day with me

[Repeat chorus 2]

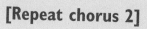

51

I heart...

Here are some more of my preferences—what are yours?

Would you rather...

1. wear a tutu or dress?
2. choose pink or purple?
3. decorate with hearts or flowers?
4. celebrate your birthday with cake or cupcakes?

⑤ play in snow or sand?

⑥ perform by singing or dancing?

Dress

Pink and purple

Hearts

Cake

Snow

Singing

kittycorn caper

Diana and Roma rescued Koko from Boris!

Got her! Boris wants to make everything boring, even Koko! Diana and Roma gave Koko an adorable teddy bear to make her feel better.

Let's bake
rainbow pancakes

Cook along with me!
Your whole family will love these
yummy, super-colorful pancakes.

Here is what you will need:

Ingredients

- ♥ 1 cup flour
- ♥ 2 tsp baking powder
- ♥ 2 tbsp sugar
- ♥ ½ tsp vanilla extract
- ♥ 1 cup milk
- ♥ 2 tbsp butter
- ♥ 1 egg
- ♥ Red, yellow, green, and blue food coloring
- ♥ Whipped cream
- ♥ Rainbow sprinkles

Now, let's start making these colorful pancakes!

1

Put the flour, baking powder, sugar, vanilla extract, milk, butter, and egg into a bowl.

2

Mix well with a whisk until smooth. Divide the batter into five bowls.

Ta-da! Let's dig in!

3

Use food coloring to dye four of them a different color, leaving one plain.

6

Shape into five circles with the back of the spoon. Cook for two or three minutes, then flip over and cook the other side until gently golden.

4

Melt a small knob of butter in a large nonstick frying pan over medium-low heat.

7

Stack the pancakes and dig in. Decorate the pancakes with whipped cream and rainbow sprinkles.

5

Once foaming, put spoonfuls of the pancake batter into the pan.

Never bake or cook without asking a grown-up for help!

Love it! Love it! Love it!

Would you rather . . .

1. have a pet vampire bat or pet slug?

2. go back in time or into the future?

3. have to stand forever or sit forever?

60